W9-ATO-623

SEEDS

To superhero grans
everywhere!
With love
TK

To the memory of
Lillian and Mary, my
very own superhero grans!
With love
JB

First US edition 2020
First published by Nosy Crow (UK) 2020

Library of Congress Catalog Card Number pending
ISBN 978-1-5362-1442-0

20 21 22 23 24 25 WKT 10 9 8 7 6 5 4 3 2 1

Printed in Shenzhen, Guangdong, China

This book was typeset in Gaspar.
The illustrations were created digitally.

Nosy Crow
an imprint of
Candlewick Press
99 Dover Street
Somerville, Massachusetts 02144

www.nosycrow.com
www.candlewick.com

SUPERHERO GRAN

TIMOTHY KNAPMAN

illustrated by

JOE BERGER

An imprint of Candlewick Press

All grandmas rock, but we know one who's **better** than the rest.

We call her our . . .

SUPERHE

RO GRAN
and she's the best!

She lives in an
amazing house that's
awesome to **explore** . . .

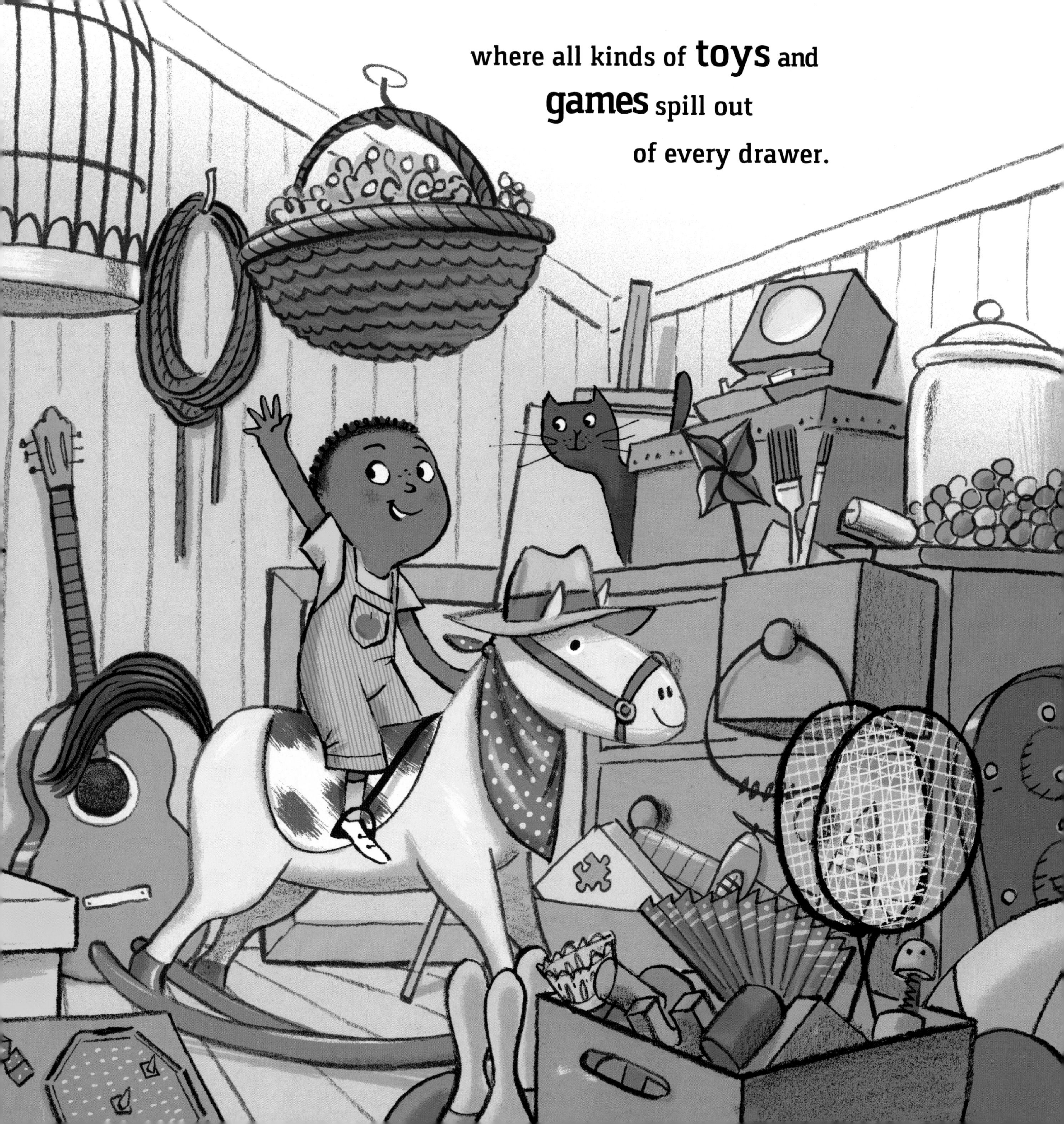

where all kinds of **toys** and
games spill out
of every drawer.

She **helps** us dress up in her glasses,
scarves and coats and hats.

Our **disguises**

are so sneaky

that we even **fool** her cats!

Then, from her makeup table,

she takes . . .

lipstick,

powder,
cream . . .

and look at us! **KA-POW!**
We make a superhero team!

She has a wondrous cookie tin
that's **always** filled with
treats,

and we never hear her say,
"Now, don't fill up
on sweets!"

She tells us **funny** stories,
and her **games** are just the **best.**
Our **favorite** is the one we call . . .

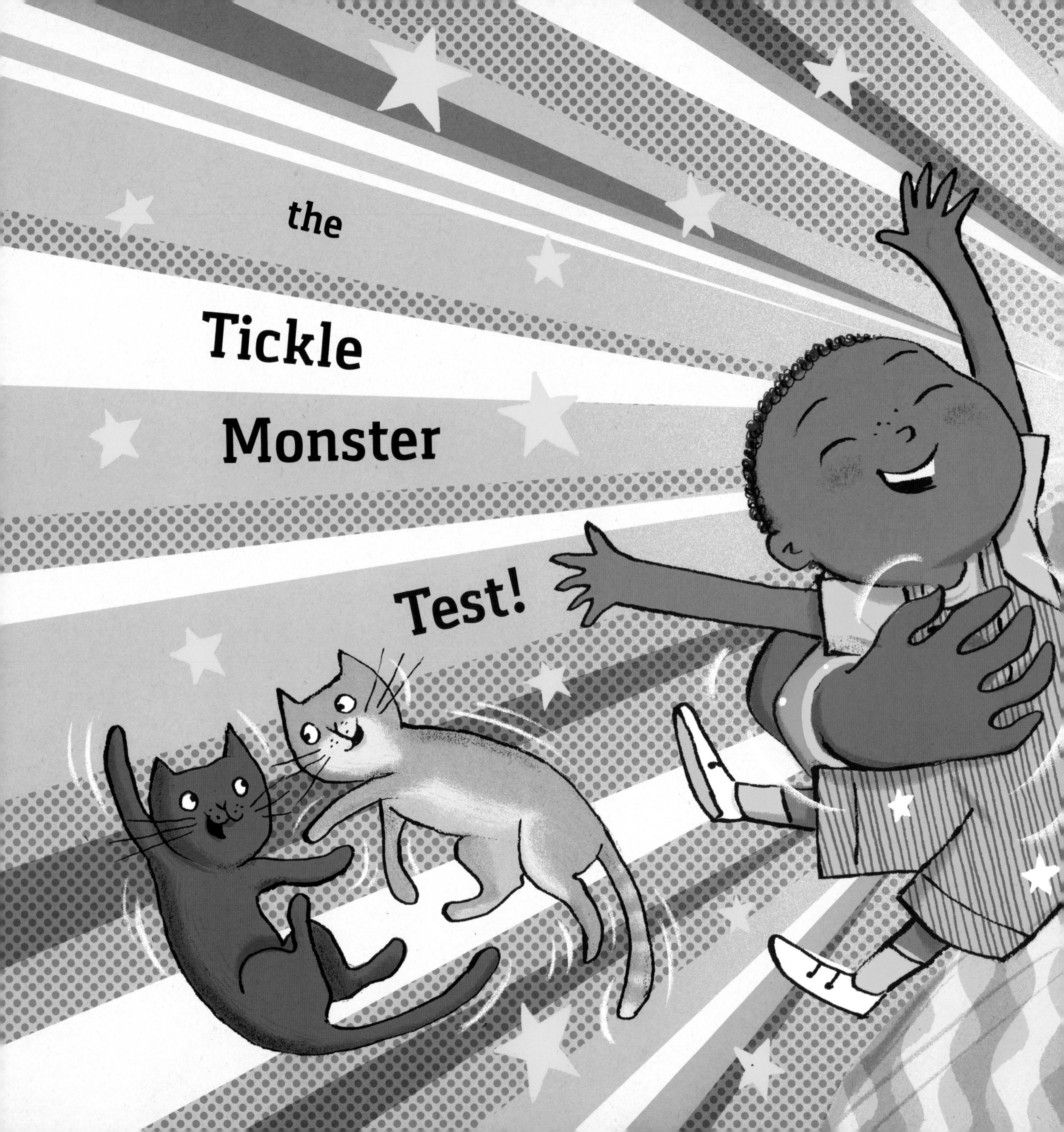
the
Tickle
Monster
Test!

She's very **good**
at gardening.

She **loves** her plants
and flowers.

They're **great** for playing hide-and-seek . . .

Gran can't find us for **hours!**

We know she can't lift buildings or go
whooshing through the sky,
but she's our **hero** just the same,
and here's the reason **why . . .**

When it's time to go back home
but we want to stay with **Gran,**
though Mom and Dad
might both say no,
our gran will have a **plan.**

She'll call up Mom and Dad and say,
"They simply **have** to stay . . .

and have a super sleepover

to end our super day."

"Oh, Gran," we say,
"how do you do the
SUPER things you do?"
She says, "Because
I love you so . . .

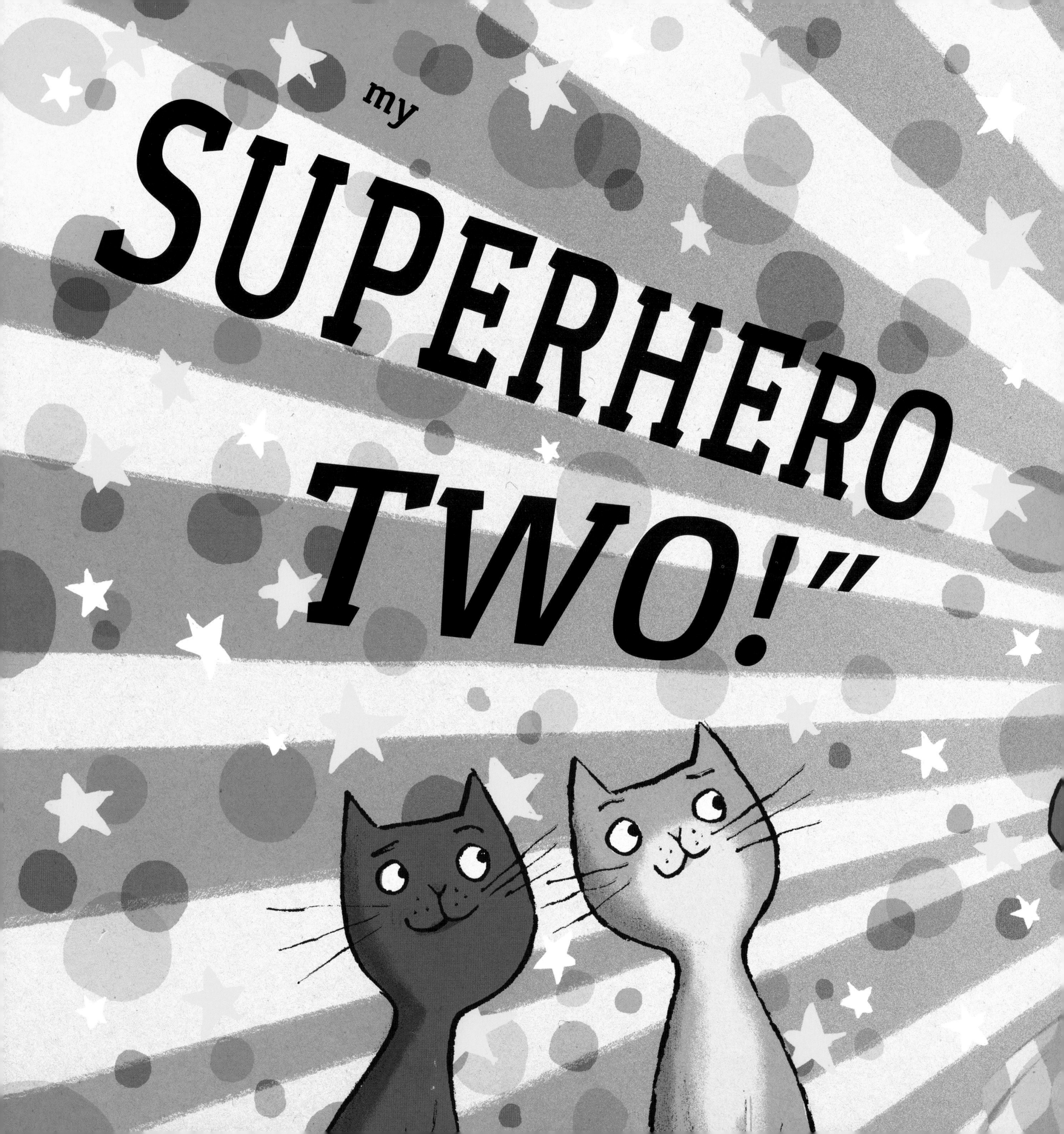
my
SUPERHERO
TWO!"